'As always, the mighty Phil Earle has written a wonderful story that does exactly what a story should do – it stays with you, it becomes part of you. Tough, funny and incredibly moving, it's a book that you'll read in one sitting, but remember for the rest of your life. From the very first word to the final full stop, *Mind The Gap* is an absolute gem.'   KEVIN BROOKS, AUTHOR OF *THE BUNKER DIARY*

'*Mind The Gap* expresses the true nature of friendship in a convincing and heartfelt manner. It lingers long after you've finished. It leaves you longing for family and hankering for friends old and new. You'll love it!' BRIAN CONAGHAN, AUTHOR OF *WHEN MR DOG BITES*

'Male friendship is portrayed in a way we seldom see in YA: intense and emotionally charged, but also warm and deeply loyal.'   THE BOOKSELLER

'It is a staggering, emotional, punch-drunk anthem to friendship and loss. It's funny and tender and raw all at once … FIVE STARS.'   WATERSTONES, REVIEWER

'It's the *Trainspotting* of the YA world, but without actual swearing or hard drugs, just references to four-letter words, cans of cider and punch-ups.'   *THE TIMES*, CHILDREN'S BOOK OF THE WEEK

First published in 2017 in Great Britain by
Barrington Stoke Ltd
18 Walker Street, Edinburgh, EH3 7LP

www.barringtonstoke.co.uk

Reprinted 2017

Text © 2017 Phil Earle

A CIP catalogue record for this book is available
from the British Library upon request

ISBN: 978-1-78112-589-2

Printed in China by Leo

Phil Earle

Mind
The Gap

Barrington Stoke

For Zoe, who I hope knows why ...

I

It's hard to sound tough when someone's hand is round your throat.

I did try, but I ended up sounding more like a choirboy than the gangster I was aiming for.

Mikey didn't bother with the tough guy act, but he didn't look scared either. He wore the same lifeless expression that he'd pinned onto his face three months ago, never letting it slip since. Not once. Not even for me.

How we'd got to this point I had no idea. Actually that's not true. I knew the *how*, what I was clueless about was the *why*.

There were some things you didn't do on our

1

estate. Steal off your own, get off with your mates' sisters (regardless of how tidy they were), and you certainly didn't get up in Trev Walker's grill.

Now I didn't have anything worth nicking, not since my grandad's old watch broke, and I doubted Mikey wanted to try it on with my brother – not with the spots that riddled Leo's skin like a furious dot-to-dot puzzle. But for some reason, today was the day that my best mate decided it was a good idea to hack off the biggest psycho this side of town.

Everyone knew who Trev was.

Everyone had at least one story they could tell about him. How he stole their car, robbed their house, or got their cousin pregnant. I wouldn't mind, but Trev was only fifteen like me and Mikey.

OK, some of the stories were the stuff of legend, passed from mouth to mouth to mouth until they were as bent as a nose that Trev had punched. But we all knew enough about Trev to realise that you still didn't mess. Hell, you didn't even make eye contact unless he made it first. And if he did make eye contact? Well, it generally meant trouble. Or pain. Or both.

So it was a mystery to me why Mikey had chosen to shoulder bump Trev. And not the sort of mystery that Scooby Doo or Sherlock Holmes would dare to tackle. Not if they liked their faces arranged as they were.

"Interesting decision," Trev whispered to Mikey. His face was a perfect pit bull snarl. "I'd have thought this path was wide enough for us all. But if it's not, then you should cross the road before trying to get past me."

Trev didn't speak like your traditional meat-head. He'd watched so many of his dad's gangster movies that he tried to talk like one of the mob.

Maybe he thought that if he was calm and polite at first, then it was OK to go on and stove your face in.

Either way, Trev hadn't liked what Mikey had done. Now Mikey had to pay.

But Mikey didn't care about the growling menace. His mask didn't move, not a single muscle in his body trembled or shook. And he certainly didn't apologise. Not even when Trev invited him to.

"There's nothing to apologise for," Mikey answered. "It was hardly a hit and run, was it? No one died. There's not a skid mark on you. Or me."

My head was on the verge of explosion. What was Mikey *doing*?

All right, he might have a quick tongue, but his fists were nowhere near as fast. Mikey had the intellect of a Porsche and the fighting skills of a Nissan Micra, and he knew it.

The hand around my throat squeezed harder. I

let out a noise I had no control over. I could smell last night's tea on the breath of the gorilla as his fist twitched again and again, like an angry dog on a lead.

"So let's try this one more time," Trev breathed. "You apologise and we move on. Simple, no?"

"No," Mikey answered, and there wasn't a smidge of emotion anywhere on his face. "No apology, and no, it's not simple either. Nothing is, where you're involved."

That was it. There was no further warning or threat, just the blur of a fist as it cannoned into Mikey's cheek. A fist that had him folding faster than the world's worst poker player.

Trev followed up with two swift kicks to the ribs and a gob of green spit, delivered with speed and power onto Mikey's head.

I wasn't daft. I knew what was coming next, but

I still flinched way too late, long after a well-aimed left hook had put me on the floor. The stamps that followed only landed on my arms, but they still branded me with a boot-shaped tattoo. I managed to close my eyes before the lungful of radioactive greb made contact with my cheek.

I lay there, balled up on the pavement. I couldn't quite believe what my best mate had gifted me. But, as Trev's crew disappeared up the street and I dared to open my eyes, all I could see was Mikey, laid up a few metres away, body shaking.

I ignored the fireworks under my cheekbones as I dragged myself over to him. I pulled my phone out and punched 999 in case the shaking was a fit or something. I'd seen it happen to a cat last year when it was knocked down by a van.

But as I fell above Mikey and rolled him over, I let the phone fall to the ground. He wasn't fitting.

He was laughing. Like he'd lost it. His whole body was shuddering with it.

I didn't know whether to join in with relief or call for the men in white coats to come and take him away.

Given what he'd been through these last three months I decided to do my duty as his friend, and I asked him if he was OK.

"OK?" he said, and he looked me in the eyes. Blood was smeared the width of his face. "What do you think?"

"You look in pain."

His body shook with another fit of laughter. His eyes and mouth were wide open, crazed, smiling, all at odds with the blood.

"Pain?" he said. "Doesn't even cover it, mate. I feel … everything."

"Everything?" I repeated. "What do you mean, everything?"

"Exactly that," he said. "I feel everything. And you know what? It feels amazing." Cue more laughter. "And better too, so much better, so much *more* than ... nothing."

As that final word fell out of Mikey's mouth and echoed down the street, it was like someone had pulled the plug on his face.

All power was lost.

The smile, the wide eyes, all gone in an instant.

Everything except the blood, that still poured off him like red sweat.

Mikey lifted a slow hand to his chin and saw the blood for the first time. But there was no reaction, no regret at what he'd done to himself, or even at what he'd done to me.

Instead, there was the return of the death mask, and after he had pinned that back in place, I was powerless to remove it.

"Come on, our kid," I said, and I pulled him to his feet. "Let's get you home, before your face falls off."

2

It wasn't just Mikey who lost someone when his dad died.

I lost someone too. I lost *Mikey*.

It's not a competition by the way, and I know I sound like a complete git to even moan about it. I mean, it's his *dad* for god's sake.

But Mikey's my best mate. And I miss him.

I could spin you a line about how he's *my brother from another mother*, but you hear that way too often for it to ever sound true. To be honest, it makes me want to gip in my mouth.

Mikey and me came up together, from day one.

I don't think I have a memory that's earlier than

us dicking around in the park with a footie, or trying to master something that would make us cool, like skateboarding. Not that we ever pulled it off. We've never managed to do anything that would make us even remotely popular. We both know our place. And we know that whatever we do, we do it in tandem.

But, if I'm honest, Mikey's always been one pace ahead of me – sharper, faster – and I've always been good with that. It doesn't make me a sheep. Or maybe it does. Either way, it's never bothered me.

What does bother me is that these last three months I've been losing him. It's like he's disappearing a bit more every day and I'm scared that soon there'll be nothing left for me to find. Not a puddle on the floor or a shadow or nothing.

It was a shock when his old man died.

I mean, people who are forty don't normally die, do they?

My mum said that men who are forty start thinking about buying a sports car that they can't get in and out of without creaking, or begin to worry about what they've been doing for the last ten years. They don't fall down in the middle of the street and not get back up again.

But then again Mikey's dad never did what anyone expected. Like sticking around for starters.

He skipped out of the front door for an audition when Mikey was seven and he didn't come back. Well, apart from the odd random day when he'd turn up at the school gates, always in a car, never the same one twice.

Mikey's dad drove them all – VWs, Saabs, Beamers. Hell, one day he turned up in a convertible Merc. All spoilers and alloys and curves. He hadn't nicked it. He had the keys for it and everything.

"Fellas!" he said, always the same greeting, always aimed at me as well as Mikey. "Been way too long. Jump in, clock's ticking."

When he turned up, two or three times a year, I always gave Mikey the chance to ditch me. Vinny wasn't *my* dad after all. But Mikey would never have it. If he was getting a ride in a decent motor, then so was I.

What followed was always the same. Laughter. From the second we closed the door, to the moment Vinny dropped us back on the edge of the estate two hours later.

I don't think it's me being all romantic, what with how he's dead now, but all we did was laugh. Big, belly-shaking rumbles that rocked your guts so hard you were in danger of following through.

There was no talk of homework or chores, just Mikey's old man riffing on anything that came into his head. And his head was always motoring.

Breaking every rule and every speed limit there was.

There was no sense or logic to a lot of it.

Sometimes I didn't even really know what he was

banging on about, but it was still funny. Mostly

because of his voice, which seemed to change with

every story he told. He had a different accent for

every one.

Sometimes his accent even changed in the

middle of a sentence. He'd start a story as David

Beckham, but finish as Nelson Mandela. I'd never

heard anything like it.

There wasn't anyone Mikey's dad couldn't

impersonate, even if he'd never met them.

"Do you reckon you could do our head teacher,

Mr Peach, Dad?" Mikey asked once.

"Course I can," his dad said. "What's he like?"

"He's one of those guys who's been old for ever,"

Mikey told him. "I reckon he was alive in the 1940s and he's still the same age now as he was then. He talks like he was born then too, like he's trying to be posh. Like he's reading the news, telling everyone that war's just broken out."

That was it. That was all Vinny needed. Thirty seconds later and old man Peach was practically in the car next to us, explaining how sports day would be run like the Dunkirk landings.

"Javelins will be thrown at first light," Vinny commanded, his face poker straight. "But only upon the General's orders. Once the enemy has been speared, then and only then, will troops long jump behind enemy lines. It will be hard, it will be bloody, but we will not stop until we have secured a glorious victory!"

That was it. He'd nailed it, leaving us helpless with laughter. We begged him to do it again and again, like we were five years old being pushed higher and higher on the swings.

By the time Vinny left us on the kerb, I was drunk. In fact, I was legless. My eyes shone like I'd been at Mum's drinks cabinet, necking the stuff that no one touches from one Christmas to the next.

And if I felt like that, who knew how hard Mikey was buzzing? It was a wonder I didn't have to race him to A&E to have his stomach pumped.

"He's an actor. You know that?" he'd say, and he wouldn't blink till the flash car had disappeared from view.

"You have mentioned it," I'd reply. There was nothing about Mikey – and his dad – I didn't know.

"He's going to be famous," Mikey would tell me. "Next job he gets is going to be on TV. Then everyone is going to know him. Know he's my dad."

I'd slap him on the back, tell him he was right. I believed it too. How could I not?

But then Vinny went and died, and his death didn't make it onto the TV.

It only just made the local paper. And that was just an advert, to tell people when and where the funeral was. And how they shouldn't bother with flowers.

It wasn't what we'd hoped for, or what Vinny or Mikey deserved, but that advert was all we had.

And, for Mikey, it was nowhere near enough.

3

I found Mikey on the roof of Mordor, 30 storeys up, feet dangling off the edge, body slumped forwards.

It sounds more dramatic than it is.

His legs might have been at the top of a drop that would splinter every bone in his body, but there was a ledge ten metres below. It would catch him if he, or anyone else dumb enough, ever thought of launching themselves off the roof.

Mordor was the ugliest building on the estate, which is really saying something when you live where we do. It was the tallest building too, which was why we'd started coming up here a couple of years ago.

I could try and tell you we came up here for the skyline, for the sunsets, to catch a glimpse of our future on the posh side of town.

But we didn't. Course we didn't. We started coming up here because we thought we stood a better chance of seeing a woman getting undressed from here. We didn't dare believe it might actually happen, but in fact, after four months of loitering, it actually did. The woman in question just happened to be 70 years old and, by the looks of it, had been wearing the same underwear since 1973.

Blinded us both it did, killed our ambition and limited our trips up here. What was the point of climbing all those stairs, or risking the piss-stinking lift, just so you could see a load of detached houses in the distance that you'd never step inside? Not unless you were there to nick the telly.

The thing that disturbed me most about finding

Mikey up on the roof of Mordor was what he was clutching. He had a bottle of Mad Dog in each hand, and one of them was almost empty.

Why he was drinking that muck I had no idea. I guessed he'd pinched it from his mum's extensive collection of "alcohol no sane person would ever touch". She could've taken it on *Antiques Roadshow* and made a fortune, or at least enough to buy a bottle of something half-decent. Something that didn't taste of bleach.

"What the hell are you drinking?" I shouted at his back.

Mikey lurched forwards in surprise. My stomach flipped, but then he turned.

"Doesn't taste too bad," he said with a sloppy grin. "If you take alternate swigs from each bottle, your brain gets confused. Could be Champagne, easy."

He waved a bottle in my face, as if to prove his

point. The sweet chemical smell of the Mad Dog mixed with the foulness coming off his breath left me frustrated. I'd already spent three hours looking for him, and I wasn't sure I had the tools to deal with him if he was properly drunk.

But I knew I had to humour him too, so I hoisted myself onto the ledge. I didn't know where to start.

"Been here long?" I asked in the end.

Mikey laughed a hollow laugh. "You aren't going to pull anyone with a line like that."

"Mate," I said. "The amount you've put away, I'm surprised you haven't tried to slip me the tongue already."

Soon as I said it I regretted it. What followed was a drunken, sitting-down tango, the end result of which was my entire face being licked. I'd rather be tongued by an old Labrador that had spent the last hour licking its balls.

"What is *in* that bottle?" I asked, feeling my stomach heave.

"Does it matter?" Mikey's grin was replaced by an expression that looked like he had trapped wind. "It does the job."

"It does if the job is smelling like a tramp."

"You'd drink it too if ..."

I waited for him to finish the sentence, half hoping he might take the chance to get stuff off his chest. But all that followed was a nasty burp, with the threat of sick to follow.

"Come on, mate," I said. "Why don't you come in now? I'll find you something to eat. Mop up the booze."

I hopped down, hoping Mikey'd follow. But he didn't. He wasn't finished.

"When was the last time we came up here together?" he asked.

"Dunno. Few months?"

"I was up here last week. I've been coming up here all the time. For ages, years. Just didn't tell you about it."

I frowned. Really? That stung a bit. There wasn't much me and Mikey didn't do together. That's how it worked.

"That right?" I asked, staying neutral. I wasn't sure if this was his drunken way of trying to start a fight.

"Not so much lately. No real point now Dad's ..."

I saw him flinch.

"... Before that, I used to come up here all the time. I'd look at the main road, you know, the by-pass near the old town, and I'd look for the poshest car I could see, and imagine Dad was driving it."

It was the first time Mikey'd said anything about

his old man in weeks, no, months, so I wasn't going to stop him.

"Ever see him?" I asked.

"Dunno. Cars are so small from up here you could crush them between your thumb and finger." He creased up his eyes and reached out his hand, pinching at a red dot on the road.

"Always made me feel better if I thought I could see him," he went on. "Meant I could be positive about how he walked out. About the fact he only bothered to turn up to see me a few times a year."

"Your old man loved you, mate," I told him, and sat back down again. "You know that. You could see it on his face, whenever he took us out."

"Not enough to stick around though, eh?"

Mikey tried to smile, and failed.

"That's why I came up here, to try and spot him," he said. He looked out as if even now he might see a car with his dad at the wheel. "I thought I could convince myself that the only reason he left was so he could land that one job that would make him famous. And when he found it, when his face was on the telly and in the papers, then he'd come back, in a *really* flash car, not one he'd borrowed, and he'd tell us that he was back. And then everyone on this poxy estate would see how amazing he was. And they'd know he was my dad."

"He would've done that too, Mikey," I said. "Course he would."

He slugged hard at his bottle, so hard that I tasted every toxic gulp as if I'd drunk it myself.

"Maybe," he said. "Maybe not. He might have run even further. Who'd blame him? Anyway, we'll never know, will we? Cos the bastard went and died."

"I don't know, mate," I said, "but maybe it's all

right to feel like that, you know?" I tried to get my words right. "My mum says it's all right to feel upset and angry at the same time. To hate him as much as you love him."

Mikey turned to look at me. The mask was still in place, but his face was stained with snot and booze.

"You know what kills me?" he said. "Know what's literally eating me up?"

I shook my head. I hadn't a clue.

"His voice," Mikey said. "I can't remember it, how it sounded. His own, not him ripping off someone else. It's gone from my brain and no matter how hard I try, I can't get it back. I can't hear my dad."

"It will come back, mate," I said. "It will. You're just upset, is all."

Mikey pulled himself to stand on the ledge, eyes firey, legs wobbling.

"But what if it doesn't?" he insisted. "What if it's gone for good? I don't think I can cope with never hearing him again. Feels like everything's ruined, like everything's gone. And if it has, then what's the point, eh? What's the point?"

He went back to the bottle. Another hard pull drained a good third, adding to his wobbliness.

I clambered beside him and took his arm before he noticed he was being led.

"We'll find it again, mate, his voice," I told him. "*I'll* find it for you if I have to. I will. I promise you."

And as I pulled him into a hug, I felt not only *his* weight, but the weight of the job in front of me.

It wasn't a mission I could fail in.

There was too much at stake.

4

Mikey's mum wore a frown like most women on the estate wore make-up.

It was smeared over every inch of her face, loud and thick.

"Oh, it's you," she said. She was clearly expecting someone else. "What do you want? He's not here. And before you ask, I've no idea where he is either. I'm not his keeper."

I could've responded with, "No, but you are his mother", but I didn't chance it. Not when I needed information out of her.

I tried not to bother Mikey's mum usually, especially after mid-afternoon when I knew she'd have had a few. But I'd got nowhere fast since I'd taken on my mission.

I thought it would be easy. It should've been when you think about it. I mean, Mikey's dad was an actor, and we're surrounded by technology. All it should've taken was a Google search to find a clip or two from something he'd acted in. An advert maybe, or a recording of a play, something I could share with Mikey that would keep his old man alive and in his ears.

But there was nothing. Nothing of use anyway. There were plenty of people with the same name, but none of them were him. I found a florist in Colorado who could make a bouquet in 49 seconds (351,052 people had watched him on YouTube) and a poker player in Australia who had lost twenty grand in a single hand. Idiot.

I did track down one actor called Vinny

Matthews, who had me air-punching when I found him. But one click later and I knew this wasn't Mikey's dad. He hadn't made *those* kind of films as far as I knew, and I didn't have time to be side-tracked.

So I drew a blank. Nothing. Not a Facebook profile, not a photo. It was like he'd never existed.

And that's what left me standing there freezing on Mikey's doorstep, breathing in the smoke from a fag that his mum had just lit.

"It's not Mikey I'm after, to be honest," I said.

"Oh yeah?" she said. "Upset you, has he? Borrowed money off you? Cos if he has you won't get it back off me. He owes me fifteen quid as it is."

I laughed, and not because she was funny – she wasn't. Fifteen quid was nothing in comparison to the fifteen years of parenting she owed Mikey, not to mention the cash she was always nicking from his pockets. I laughed because I had to keep her sweet until she gave me what I needed.

"So what is it then?" she said. "What do you want? I've things to do, you know?"

I bit my lip again. She was wearing a silky dressing gown and fluffy slippers, and there were cig burns on both. She didn't exactly look like she was ready to perform urgent open-heart surgery. She didn't even look ready to wash the dishes – not that she ever managed that either.

"It's about your Mikey," I said. "Well, about Vinny really."

She slammed the door, hard, brutally. But my foot was in the way and I swore, a short, harsh word that she used far more often than me.

"What did you leave your leg there for?" she yelled, looking at the door for damage.

"I didn't know you were going to try and amputate it, did I?" I yelled back.

I hopped backwards and forwards, but had no idea why – it did nothing for the pain.

"Yeah, well what do you expect, coming here, spouting his name?" She almost spat the words out.

"I need your help," I said, trying to keep the pleading note out of my voice. "Was hoping you might have something that belonged to him. Something I could give to Mikey. Something that might help him. Help Mikey get over him ... dying."

I didn't need to be so worried about using the 'D' word. It might have upset Mikey, but it didn't dent his mum's armour.

"Best thing our Mikey can do is forget all about him," she said. "Worked for me."

"But it's not as easy for Mikey, is it?" I said. "No

matter what Vinny did, he was still his dad. And now he's gone."

"Yeah, well, I can't help, can I?" she said. "I haven't got nothing. Vinny didn't have much to start with, and anything he did leave behind, I burned."

I could believe that. Either that or she'd have sold it. Both were possible.

"You haven't got a photo, or a letter, or even a film of anything he made?" I asked. "Something with his voice on?"

She laughed. A gravelly, sneering laugh. "Anything he made? That bloke couldn't make a bed, never mind a film. Mikey'd do well to remember that. Do well to remember that Vinny walked out on us too. Years ago."

I'd heard enough. Too much, in fact. How she could be in any way related to my best mate I didn't know. But I wasn't giving up on Mikey, or Vinny.

She was a right cow but she was the only lead I had.
So I fought back.

"Did it hurt?" I asked, forcing my voice to be
calm. It was a random enough question to stop her
closing the door on me again.

"What?" she said. "When?"

"When they whipped your heart out," I said.
"Must have stung a bit, especially when they clearly
did it without anaesthetic."

"Now you listen to me," she began. "You little –"

"No, you listen," I said, getting up in her face.
"It might suit you to be pissed up and numb, but it
doesn't suit your Mikey. His dad's dead. His dad's
dead and it's killing him, every day it's killing him.
Bit by bit. Now you might *think* you don't mind
being on your own, but if you lose Mikey too, then
what have you got, eh? Nothing. You've got nothing.
And neither have I."

I stopped myself there and I didn't wait for her to respond. What was the point? She clearly didn't have it in her to help.

But I'd only gone a dozen steps when I heard her in my ear.

"South Bank!"

It was so clear that it sounded like she was sat on my shoulder, when in fact she hadn't moved an inch from the doorstep.

She shouted it again.

South Bank.

It was enough to make me turn round. Enough for her to shuffle towards me in her slippers.

"He ... Vinny, he used to perform on the South Bank," she said, and she pulled her dressing gown tight around her. "Street theatre. Juggling with knives, stuff like that. Always seemed a shame he never managed to stab himself ... anyway. He worked with another fella. He might be able to help you."

"What was his name?" I wanted it out of her before she changed her mind.

"How the hell would I know?" she spat. "All I know is he had a Mohican. Green it was. Exactly the sort of idiot Vinny always hung about with."

And that was it. Off she walked, even though I'm sure she must've had a broom in the flat that she could've flown on.

I didn't hang about. I didn't shout "thank you" or "bye" or anything else. It was way too late to be matey. And, besides, I had to be somewhere else. I was already legging it to the South Bank.

5

The South Bank was rammed. The sun was out,
pulling every tourist and resident like a magnet
onto its length. It was all a bit much to be honest.
Fine if you had all day to wander along the river,
point at the wonders of London and lick at an
ice cream. But I didn't. I had to find this street
performer.

As I squeezed my way through the crowds, I felt
lucky that I had a green Mohican to work with. I just
had to hope he changed his hairstyle less often than
Mikey changed his clothes.

There'd been no sign of Mikey. I'd looked for
him as I dashed to jump on the train, in the hope he

might be up for coming with me. He loved the South Bank. But he'd gone underground.

I asked a few likely suspects if they'd seen or spoken to him, but there was nothing to go on. One lad had spotted him going into the off-licence, but hadn't seen him come out. I ran in to check, expecting to find him in a stupor among a dozen empty cans of cider. But he wasn't there. Wherever he was, I just had to hope he was OK, and hopefully now at ground level instead of on top of Mordor.

So that's what left me here, on my own, weaving past idiots wearing huge Union Jack hats and waving cameras that were bigger than our flat.

At least it was easy to spot where the street performers were. All you had to do was follow the crowd as they buzzed and whooped. Not that you could blame them. I'd always been a sucker for a show too, but I could never understand why people so daring and sickeningly talented were flogging themselves for pennies, when other guys who can barely walk in a straight line earn mega bucks in Las Vegas.

I'd like to see Britney Spears swallow a sword while she juggles four flaming torches.

I trailed from crowd to crowd. It was crappy dragging myself away from all the performers, but I couldn't see a Mohican of any colour, and I knew I had to keep moving until I did.

I must have walked from the Eye to the National Theatre a dozen times before at last I caught a flash of green that wasn't on someone's jumper or rucksack. This was perched like an untidy parrot on top of someone's head, and it had me bouncing through the crowd with a new, unexpected energy.

It was him, it had to be – and, man, did he know how to work a crowd. He had them hanging on his every word, his every movement. They laughed and gasped on demand, even when he was doing nothing more than walking round the chalk circle that was his stage.

It was so simple. All I had to do was wait until the end of the show, slip a quid into his hat and this man would gift me Vinny, or some part of him, and that would bring my friend back to planet Earth.

But after a couple of minutes of watching Mr Mohican's show, I felt something. A twitch in my pocket – fleeting, but enough for me to clock it and know exactly what was going on.

There had been a hand in there, and it didn't belong to me. It was a hand that was riffling for anything it could find. Well, that was a laugh for starters. I wasn't a complete mug like most of the tourists beside me. There was no wallet in my pocket, no phone or keys or anything that might be of any interest, unless the owner of the mystery hand collected ancient Mars bars wrappers or crumpled packs of Rizla.

I didn't let on. I had no idea how big this person was. They could be an eight-foot gorilla with spiky brass knuckle-dusters for all I knew. Until I knew, I wasn't going to cause a fuss. Instead, I turned my head a touch to the left, and watched a lanky streak of a lad wind his way past me. He didn't even break his stride as his left hand snaked into the pocket of a woman who was taking a photo. A second later, his hand was out again and the sun glinted off a phone which then disappeared up his sleeve.

The speed with which it happened was mad – so mad I had to keep watching as the Streak pulled the same trick another two times in thirty seconds. At this rate, he'd be eating steak every night for a month. Hell, by Christmas he could retire to his own private island in the Caribbean.

I was so impressed that I ended up watching him instead of the main event. I found myself applauding him instead of Mr Mohican when the show ended.

'Come on,' I told myself. 'Focus. Remember what you're here for.'

And I waited as Mr Mohican addressed the crowd one last time.

"Ladies and gentlemen," he said, "boys and girls, if you've enjoyed the performance, and I know you have, then please do show it in the time-honoured fashion. To see wonders like this in the West End would set you back a mint, so when my friend here passes the hat around, please leave your coins in your pocket and give me something I can fold into my wallet instead. I've been the Green Goblin and you've been ... well, you're about to be extremely generous!"

He bowed, low and deep, showing the green stripe of his hair. I took a step towards him, only to be stopped by someone thrusting a sailor's hat in my face.

"No coins," a voice said. The voice came from the streaky lad who'd spent the last ten minutes pick-pocketing the contents of an Apple store out of the crowd's pockets.

Hilarious. It could only mean one thing. Mr Mohican – aka the Green Goblin – and the Streak were in it together. The Goblin was there to distract them while his partner in crime collected some *serious* wedge to supplement the offerings in the sailor's hat. I should've congratulated him there and then, but was too stunned.

"Sorry. I've got nothing." It wasn't a lie, but the Streak still fixed me with a look that could've dented steel. "But my dad has," I added and pointed to a guy a few metres down, who was way too young and good-looking to share any of my genes.

But it was enough to send the Streak sliding on his way, leaving me to approach the Green Goblin, who was now gathering up his props.

"Top show." I smiled, before pointing at his partner and adding, "And I have paid."

He smiled back at me, without a hint of charm or warmth. I suppose there was no need to waste his energy on me if I'd already coughed up.

"Don't try it at home, eh?" he said.

"Nah," I said. "I can't cut me own toenails without drawing blood."

He looked at me like I was a total plank.

"Right."

I had to do this fast. "Listen," I said. "I'm sorry to bother you, it's just I'm looking for someone."

"Police are usually over there." He waved the juggling club in his hand to dismiss me.

"Oh, they can't help," I said, and my voice was as cold as his. "See, this person is already dead, and I think you might've known them. Hope so anyway."

He really did think I was mad now. "Think I had something to do with it, do you?" he said. "Cos if you're a cop, you're the weirdest one I've ever seen. And I've seen some weirdos."

"Cop? Me? As if." I tried to laugh it off. "No, it's just ... it's my mate's dad who's died, and my mate's falling apart and I thought you, well, I thought you might be able to help."

"Well, I can't bring him back," he said. "I'm a cracking magician, but I do have my limits ..."

He wasn't going to distract me with his snide jokes. "No, it's just you knew him," I went on. "He was a friend, you performed with him. And I thought you might have something that would help my mate. Doesn't have to be much. A video of you both doing your stuff would be amazing."

I'd chosen my words with care – I hoped if I put it well, my speech might tug a bit at his emotions. But this goblin wasn't for bending. Not one bit.

"You should be on the telly, pal," he said. "Bring the house down with sob stories like that." He tried to end it there, but I refused to be fobbed off, staring at him until he sighed.

"Come on then, who are we talking about?"

Brilliant. This was the moment the plan fell into place.

"Vinny Matthews."

His look turned from irritated to murderous. "This conversation is over," he said. "Jog on."

I never was much of a runner.

"You did know him then?" I said.

"I said, game over." He looked half a metre taller all of a sudden and quite a lot broader, but I wasn't going to back down now. I couldn't. All I could think of was Mikey. My mate. How much he needed this.

"Look, I don't need a reference from you or nothing," I said, and I forced myself to look him in the eye. "It's just my mate, Vinny's son, he's struggling. Can't cope that his dad has gone. Wants to hear his voice again. All I need is a clip. Five seconds even. Something that gives him his dad back. You can do that, can't you? You must've recorded some of your shows on your phone, eh?"

"You really think I'd give that scumbag memory space?" His shaved head was getting redder, and fast. "I don't even want to give him headspace, not that I have much choice. Not after what he did."

"Why?" I jumped in. "What did he do?" I wasn't

actually sure I wanted to know. This was starting to smell pretty sour. It was starting to reek.

And then the Green Goblin lifted his right hand and I saw it, or rather I didn't. There was a gap where most of his middle and index fingers should've been.

"It wasn't exactly brain surgery, what I asked him to do," he said. "It wasn't like *he* had to juggle with the chainsaw. All he had to do was throw it correctly to me."

My brain filled in the rest as my Co-op sandwich lurched up into my throat.

"You have any idea how hard it is for me to juggle now?" he said. "Any idea how long I had to retrain? Any idea how much money I missed out on because of that turd? So forgive me if I don't help you and your mate. Forgive me if I do a little dance when I hear that Vinny's dead. So go on, son, move on, before I call a cop over and say you've been dipping your hand in my hat."

I couldn't quite believe what I'd heard, and I didn't want to picture chainsaws and hands and missing fingers. But at the same time I wasn't going to *move on*. Because, by talking of the police, the green-haired idiot had dug himself a mighty deep grave.

"Yeah, why don't we do that?" I challenged. "Bring a cop over and I'll tell them all about what your mate there has in his pockets, and how you work together to fill them."

"Don't know what you're talking about," he blustered, losing his cool for the first time.

"Well, there's nothing to worry about then is there?" I said, and I made as if to head for the coppers.

He grabbed at my sleeve. "Listen," he said. "I

haven't got nothing on Vinny. Nothing. Not a video, not an answer phone message, nothing."

"Then it was nice meeting you. Enjoy prison," I called over my shoulder. "Plenty of time to practise your juggling in there I reckon."

The coppers were getting closer but I held my nerve. The Goblin had to have something. He *had* to.

Five paces.

Four.

Three.

Two.

"Wait!"

I stopped.

Please, please?

"There is one thing," his urgent voice hissed in my ear. "A person you could try. Someone who knew Vinny. Reckoned he was his agent."

"Go on."

"This bloke – he's got an office off the Strand. Upstairs from the chemist's on the corner. Sid, his name is. Second name starts with an S too. Silversmoke or something."

I didn't say thanks. It wasn't like he'd offered the info out of kindness or as a favour.

Instead I looked at him. Hard.

"Sid had better exist," I told him. "Because if he doesn't, I know where you live."

And with that, I strode off like a cowboy, making for the bridge that led to the Embankment, and onto the Strand.

6

I strode across the bridge full of hope.

The Goblin might not have offered up exactly
what I wanted, but he hadn't slammed the door shut
either. And I had to admit that the new lead was
a good one, probably the best yet. If anyone was
going to have evidence of Vinny's existence it was
his agent. Photos definitely, but surely he'd have
something on film too? An audition piece or an ad,
anything that I could put in front of Mikey and plug
into his ears.

It seemed easy, so easy, and the thought of it
drove me across the Thames, despite the irritation
of a swarm of tourists buzzing the other way.

But as I hit the steps down to Embankment station, my phone buzzed in my pocket. The screen told me that Mikey was calling. I shoved a finger in my other ear to drown out the mayhem of the crowd as I answered, but I still couldn't hear him properly.

"Mikey? That you, mate?"

It was. I could hear him, just, but he wasn't talking to me. His voice was muffled and shouty, and I could hear the alcohol sloshing around inside him.

"You wanna know something?" he was yelling. "You wanna know the truth? You're a joke, mate. Everyone knows it. Behind your back they all shout it. Know who's a joke? That Trev Walker."

I let out a howl, which parted the sea of tourists pretty fast. What was he doing, the idiot? Had he learned nothing? I tried to make sense of it. But I could only suppose that his phone was in his pocket and he'd called me by accident while he ranted at Trev.

I shouted down the phone. I told him to back off, run, stick his *own* fist in his mouth, anything that would stop him talking.

But he didn't hear me. Course he didn't. He was still yelling at Trev, calling him every name under the sun, along with a lot of words you won't find in any dictionary.

What should I do now? I could jump on the Tube and then a bus, but by then Trev would've done his worst.

No, even if I dashed home, and picked Mikey and his broken teeth up off the floor, I couldn't make all the other bruises disappear.

In desperation, I ended the call and tried to phone him back.

Nothing. It rang then went to voicemail.

I tried again. And again.

Then on the seventh attempt, I got nothing *but* the voicemail. What did that mean?

Had Trev stamped on Mikey's mobile as well as his head, his hands and everything else? It was possible. What was clear was that there was nothing I could do about it. I was powerless.

Well, almost powerless.

In front of me, the road climbed to the Strand. And on the Strand was an office with a guy who might have just the medicine that Mikey needed.

Did I plough on or dash for home? Choosing was agony.

I called Mikey one last time.

Voicemail.

I couldn't reach him.

And that summed it up. I hadn't managed to get through to Mikey in months. And I needed to, desperately. So I gave it no more thought and dashed on to find Sid the agent.

O

I didn't know what I expected an agent's office to be like, but it wasn't this. I expected it to be flash, bling, all glass and stainless steel with beautiful and talented people milling about. But instead I got plastic, chipboard, and a guy who looked more like a dodgy landlord.

Sid was bald, grubby and fat, his gut straining against the button that held up his trousers. I frowned at him like he was a mistake, and to be fair he didn't look too pleased to see me either.

That could've been to do with the lie I told to get into his office. In my head, it had been a good idea to pass myself off as a courier, but when I arrived empty-handed and breathless after sprinting up six flights of stairs, Sid didn't look too chuffed. If I'd lugged a massive pizza up there I reckon he might have adopted me, but I had nothing to offer. In fact, I could barely speak.

"You the agent?" I gasped. I couldn't help but hope he was the cleaner, although it was clear he'd been nowhere near soap or water in weeks.

"I am," he said. "But you don't look much like a courier to me."

"Why's that?"

"Because couriers tend to have something to deliver. Now I don't know what you want, but unless you can whistle the national anthem out of your backside, then I don't want to know. Novelty arse whistlers I can make money out of. Ugly little gits like you, I can't."

There was a pause, like he almost expected me

to drop my jeans and belt out a tune. Then, when I didn't move, Sid told me to let myself out and turned back towards his office.

"I need your help!" I shouted after him. It made no difference. He kept on walking. "It's important," I yelled. "It's about one of your actors. Who's died."

That was enough to grab his attention. He must have thought it was going to cost him money. How could he take a cut of someone's earnings when they were no longer breathing?

"Oh hell." He sighed. "It's not Tina, is it? I just lent her the money to have her teeth done for that soap audition."

"No, it's not her," I said. I couldn't help but feel sorry for Tina, working with such a scumbag. "It's Vinny. Vinny Matthews."

And that's when things turned primeval. That's when Sid turned from a grubby sloth into an

Olympic sprinter. Micro-seconds after I had uttered Vinny's name, I was pinned against the wall with Sid's hands around my throat.

This was happening way too often for my liking.

"You burst into my office," Sid spat, "pretending to have a parcel, lying like the scally that you are, then you dare to say *his* name. Give me one good reason why I shouldn't dangle you out the window by your shoe laces."

"Because I'm his son's best mate," I gasped. It wasn't much of an explanation but it was all I had. "And Vinny's death is killing his son. I thought you could help, cos you're his agent. Thought you might have a tape of him, a video, something I could give to Mikey."

Sid's eyes bored into me. "Now you listen, you little scrote," he said. "I don't care who you are and I don't care about this Mikey. That scumbag

Matthews cost me. More than anyone else I ever met. I got him gigs. Plenty of them. But he let me down, every time." Sid's grip on me grew tighter. "He didn't show up. Or he turned up drunk. He'd argue with directors, tell them they were wrong, try it on with everyone from producers to make-up girls. The only time he made any money was those bloody voice-overs, and he never passed a penny of it on to me."

"But he's dead," I said. "Can't you forgive him?"

"Forgive him?" Sid was snarling now. "You're lucky I don't make you take me to his boy so I can collect on his debts. You've got ten seconds. Ten seconds to get down those stairs and out my door. If I can hear, or see, or smell you after that, then you'll be taking your food through a tube for the rest of your days. You'll be wishing YOU were Vinny Matthews."

That was my cue to run. I knew that. But I was desperate. I couldn't leave yet.

"Please, Sid," I almost begged. "Just give me one thing. One tiny thing and you'll never see me again."

And that's when he started to deliver on his promise. The man was fat. There was no doubt about that. But he was fat and strong. I realised that when his fist embedded itself first in my cheek, then in my guts.

There aren't words to describe it. Pain doesn't come close. Made what happened with Trev and his gang look like handbags at dawn. Never mind fireworks, bombs went off in my skull.

"Didn't you hear me?" Sid spat. "Perhaps you can hear me now?" His fist connected again. "What about now?" *Whack.* "Or now."

I was reeling like a four year old on a bike with no stabilisers.

I reached for the wall and found it, but it seemed to shuke me off. I had to get out. I had to, but my mouth wouldn't listen. I couldn't go back to Mikey with nothing.

"Just a tape," I whimpered. "A video. Anything. For my mate. Don't you understand? He's my best mate."

But this meant nothing to Sid, who batted and swiped at me with his fists until I was back out the door. The stairs loomed, mouth open, ready to swallow me whole. With one last powerful left hook, Sid sent me tumbling down them, all the way to the first landing.

"If I come back out and find you still lying there, then ... well, you don't need me to tell you what'll happen, do you?"

The door slammed shut, shadowing Sid behind the glass.

That was it. Game over.

I had to go home with nothing.

I hoped Mikey was in better shape than me.

7

I could see Embankment station a hundred metres away, but my legs refused to take me there.

I was damaged, wrecked. I was bleeding from a cut by my right eye, while my ribs felt like someone had played xylophone on them with a sledge hammer.

It wasn't just Sid's fists that had hurt me. It was his hard-hearted refusal to help. He'd left me with nothing, and that left Mikey with nothing, and that sent a pain round my body that was impossible to carry. So I slumped in the doorway of a fancy gallery while my blood dripped onto the floor like the grimmest piece of pavement art.

People raced past, frowning at the state of me, swerving like I had the plague. One guy with a posh camera snapped off a load of pictures. I didn't even have the energy to growl at him, much as he would've loved it. Would've added to the raw drama of it or something.

What should I do next? I should probably have gone to hospital, but I had no idea where the nearest one was. And, anyway, that would be admitting defeat.

I remembered Mikey. I had to try and call him again.

My phone's screen was smashed, reflecting a fractured, bloodied image of myself. Not exactly the sort of screensaver I was after.

I called Mikey's number.

Still voicemail.

I thought about leaving a message, but wasn't

sure what I'd say or whether he'd understand a word of it. I could feel my lips swelling like I'd been ambushed by wasps. My brain didn't feel far behind.

I needed to get home, but there was nothing in my legs. Only when a kid came up and offered me a fistful of change from his dad's pocket did I see a reason to get back up on my feet.

If I didn't get back to Mikey and find a way of getting through to him, it could be him soon, sitting on the streets, accepting hand-outs, bleeding into a drain.

I tried to smile at the kid, and his dad, as they pulled me to my feet. Then I pointed at a guy who was way more in need of £1.68 than I was. I had my Oyster card to get me home, and that would do, I told myself, as I limped towards the Tube.

The madness of rush hour was kicking in. People poured into the station from every direction, elbows sharp, the merest bump threatening to bowl me over.

I needed a drink. A drink and a comfy bed, in that order.

'Focus,' I told myself. Zone out and get home, like everyone else was doing. I allowed the crowd to swallow me, carry me down the escalator to the south-bound platform.

But the deeper I travelled, the hotter it got. It felt like I was being roasted, like I was descending into the fires of hell. The heat hit me everywhere, stinging my cuts and swelling my brain, scrambling my ability to think or stand up.

As the escalator ran out, so did my strength. I fell to my knees, and others behind me tumbled over the top, their knees and feet battering my head.

They spat and swore. Kids were pulled away from me in disgust and fear. None of it registered.

None of it mattered. All that mattered was getting on that train and riding south.

I used the wall as a crutch and limped on, squinting past blood until I saw the south-bound sign. There was a sea of people waiting on the platform, but no one wanted to get too close and so they left me more space than I needed or deserved.

I squinted to see when the next train was.

One minute.

I had to get on it, even if the carriage was bursting. I had to get off this platform. I'd be all right as long as I was moving, heading home.

"Scuse me," I grunted, trying to get as close to the yellow line as I could, guessing where the doors would stop. "Scuse me, ta."

People parted.

Amazing how looking like a battle-weary bum made me so powerful.

I could hear the train coming down the tunnel. Rumbling, pounding, echoing inside my head, making my cuts and bruises throb. I clutched my ribs, but they shook under my fingers, the pain shocking, fizzing into my hand. All I could do was take deep breaths and swallow the constant rise of bile in my throat.

The noise grew louder, harsher. I craned my neck and the light from the train's cab hit me, burning my eyeballs. It hurt, killed, but I stared on as it kept me awake. I told myself –

Wait till the doors open, get on at all costs, seat or no seat.

The train came to a stop while its brakes shrieked a note of despair. All I could smell was heat and burning and dirt, but it didn't matter, it didn't matter because the doors were opening, the doors were opening and a man's voice was greeting me.

"This is Embankment station. Please mind the gap."

He was helping me, telling me what I needed to know, giving me permission to get on board, to escape. But for some reason my brain betrayed me, rooted me to the spot, even when all the passengers had got off.

This didn't go down well behind me.

"Come on, mate."

"Get on, will you?"

"Push past. He's not all there, is he?"

Their words bounced off me. I didn't care, not even when they jostled and shoved and elbowed me, setting fire to my bruises all over again.

I was staying exactly where I was.

I had to.

Ten seconds before, all I could think about was getting on that train, but now all I wanted was to wait for the next one.

To be sure.

Because, if I was right, in those last ten seconds, everything had changed.

8

We shuffled like a couple of old lads on the way to collect their pensions from the post office.

I could only guess from the way he was walking that Mikey's injuries were as bad as mine.

He winced with each step, which made me wonder if Trev Walker had whipped the soles of his feet as well as every other bit of his body.

I'd trawled every low spot on the estate, places you wouldn't enter in daylight let alone at night, before I found Mikey. It would've saved me time – and energy I didn't have after a kicking from a sadistic showbiz agent – if I'd just waited outside the off-licence for him all along.

Because that was where I clocked him, pounding on the shutters, eyes swollen shut, knuckles grated and bleeding. As plans go, his wasn't awful. He wanted booze, though he would've been wiser to try four hours earlier when the shop was still open.

"Mikey, mate," I said, not wanting to shock him as I approached from behind. He didn't hear, just started rapping louder, so I laid a hand that was meant to be comforting on his shoulder.

Massive error.

He spun round with a wild right hook that opened my eye again.

I folded to the floor, Mikey on top of me, his eyes on fire. I had no idea what he'd been drinking, but he was so out of it, it could've been something he'd found in the cupboard under the sink.

"Mikey," I gasped from behind my own raised fists. "Mikey, it's me, you tool. It's ME!"

But Mikey didn't want to listen, or couldn't. Which left me with no option but to fight back. It killed me to do it. Fifteen years as brothers without so much as a Chinese burn between us, and here I was, working out where to lamp him to bring him to his senses.

To be honest, I could've hit him anywhere. His body was a purple mass of damage. A single punch to the cheek had him rolling off me and panting for air.

"Mikey, it's me, you idiot," I yelled. "Listen. Listen. LISTEN TO ME! It's all right, mate. I promise you. It's all going to be all right."

O

Looking back, which is difficult given how wrecked we were, it was lucky I found Mikey when I did.

Our estate was not a forgiving place, and neither were most of the people who lived on it, especially the ones still on the streets at three in the morning. All it would've taken was the wrong word to the wrong face and Mikey would've become a permanent part of the pavement. Instead I dragged him across it, all the way back to my flat.

There was no way I was taking him home to his mum, and I didn't care if we woke my dad. I pulled Mikey into the shower, clothes still on, and heaved him under the jets. I didn't care if he drank the water or washed in it, as long as it brought him back from wherever he was. It sort of did. He recognised me, at last, but he wasn't too happy when he came face to face with reality.

"Best jeans," he slurred. "Cost me a fortune ..."

"Well, they're already shredded, so get over yourself," I replied, wrapping him in the biggest roughest towel we owned and marching him to my room.

The sight of a bed unlocked something new in him, a need, not to argue or fight, but to sleep. Within seconds of me shepherding him onto the mattress he was gone. His snores battled with Dad's from the room next door. Only after I'd rolled him onto his side and placed a bin below his mouth, did I allow myself to relax. My ribs groaned like Sid's fists were still buried in them.

I should've showered too. I should've shown myself the same care I'd shown Mikey, but it didn't seem important. Besides, I'd used all the hot water on him and now my body was crying for sleep as well. So I lay on a pile of laundry like it was a king-size bed and I let go. I didn't feel a thing until the next morning.

O

The next morning brought few positives – hangovers (for some), bruises, faces crusted to pillows with blood, and the painful memory of Sid snarling as he unloaded his fists at me.

I hoped Mikey had been too hammered to remember what Trev had done to him.

The only positive I could take from it was that we'd slept so long we'd missed rush hour, so could get back to Embankment in peace. Well, we could if Mikey would agree to it.

"You what?" he said when I asked him to come with me. "No chance. Upright I might manage, but uptown? Not today."

"You've got to," I told him. "There's something you need to see."

"Mate, there's nothing up there but tourists and

suits," he said. "Neither of which will sort out my headache." He rammed the bloody pillow over his head, but I removed it with the neatest of swipes.

"And what are you going to do instead, eh?" I asked. "Get hammered again? Walk up to Trev with a baseball bat and hand it to him, then get down on your knees?"

"Sounds better than being dragged up West by you."

"Jesus, Mikey, listen to yourself," I said, starting to rage. "Do you really think I want to do this any more than you? It's not just you who got lumps kicked out of them yesterday. I did too. One of my ribs feels like it's taken root in my lung, and it's all because I've been trying to sort things out. For you. To drag you back. And I think I've done it. So for god's sake, take your head out from up your arse, and do what you need to do. I'm out of here in half an hour, and you're coming with me. Even if I have to drag you out the door by the balls."

As speeches go, it was hardly Winston Churchill fighting them on the beaches, but it worked.

O

Just two hours later Mikey and I were at the entrance to Embankment station.

"Do we have to go down there?" Mikey said. He was trying to hide his black eyes behind a pair of Dad's old sunglasses. It was a miserable attempt – a bucket might have just about covered them, but the glasses didn't. "If we have to go any further can't we just get another bus?" he moaned.

I shook my head. "Has to be here, mate. But I promise I won't make you set foot on a train."

"Then why are we even going down there? Jesus, this is stupid."

Mikey was on the verge of losing it, and I couldn't let that happen. Not now. Not when we were so close.

"Look, trust me, will you?" I said. I'd have looked him in the eye if it weren't for the stupid shades. "There's something down there for you. Something that's going to help. Do this one thing for me, and if it doesn't help, then I'll buy you a bottle of that killer Mad Dog and we can go home and get properly smashed."

I wasn't joking either. If this didn't pay off, then there really was no hope left.

I grabbed Mikey and pulled him into the station, towards the ticket barriers.

9

Mikey dragged his heels like a kid being forced into a shop to buy salad instead of a bag of sweets.

"This is crap," he moaned. "Why the hell are you dragging me down here if we're not even getting on a train?"

I coughed. The dust and muck wafting from the platforms was niggling my head, and it was crusty enough already.

"Stop your moaning, will you?" I growled.

We slouched on the right-hand side of the escalators, leaving the left for the try-hards and the tourists who didn't know any better.

With shaking hands, I pulled out my phone and

looked up an email that reminded me that I wasn't doing this for nothing. Far from it.

I took a deep breath, one eye on Mikey in case he decided he'd had enough. The metal step vibrated beneath me and spat us onto the ground at the bottom.

"Up here," I said, leading Mikey. "South-bound platform."

"We've just come from the south ..."

"Trust me, will you. Please?"

I herded him down the south-bound tunnel, my eyes flitting to the electronic board as soon as it came into view.

Delays. Minor ones, but ones that meant a four-minute wait instead of two. My insides itched with impatience, but I kept it hidden. Mikey, on the other hand, prowled along a two-metre stretch of platform until he'd almost worn the concrete out, and gave the eye of death to anyone who dared look at him.

"Calm down, mate?" I said.

"You calm down," he spat. "I'm hurting here and for some funny reason this place isn't helping."

He was hurting? My insides were trashed too, but I didn't let his attitude get to me. Instead I watched as the timer clicked down to two minutes. A hundred and twenty seconds. Not long, but long enough for me to have to work hard to keep Mikey on side.

"When the train arrives get as close to the doors as you can, but you don't need to get on," I told him. "You just need to listen, understand?"

"Listen? Listen to what?" he snarled. "Mate, this is bollocks. I'm out of here."

He turned and made for the way we came. He only stopped when I got right in his way.

"Mikey, please," I begged. "It's not bollocks. Two minutes. Less even."

"Get out of my way."

I didn't move.

"Don't make me put you on your arse."

I still didn't move.

I saw the timer behind him flick to a minute. I put my hands on his shoulders to root him.

"Last warning."

Mikey's eyes flared just as they had when he'd squared up to Trev, but like Trev, I wasn't scared. There was no point. Help was on its way. The headlight of the Tube train was sparking up the tunnel, a dirty breeze washing over us.

All I had to do was hold him, thirty more seconds, forty tops, then he'd know, then it would be OK.

Only problem was, Mikey hadn't read my script and he chose that moment to push hard. My arms flew off his shoulders as I skittered backwards, taking out a guy in a suit before I hit the deck.

I pulled myself to my feet, the roar in my head as loud as the one screaming from the train. Mikey was lumbering to the exit, limping and panting, but there was no way I was going to let him make it.

Within seconds I was a shadow's length behind him. By the time the train pulled to a stop, my arms were wrapped around his neck, backing him up, ignoring his struggle.

"You need to listen to this, Mikey, you hear me?" I shouted in his ear. "I've found it. Everything you asked me to find. Stop being a dick, and listen. For Christ's sake, LISTEN."

I gripped his throat harder as I pulled him closer to the train doors. I didn't like squeezing like that but I had to so he would listen to what I had heard.

The train wheezed to a halt and I dragged him

to the right, keeping up with the double doors, scattering anyone in our path like skittles. I didn't dare let go, not even a little, not until the voice spoke. Not until Mikey heard.

"Listen!" I demanded, and for a second I squeezed even harder. The voice cut in as the doors hissed open.

This is Embankment station. Please mind the gap.

It must have only been two seconds long, that announcement, all eight words of it, but when I heard it again, I wanted to explode. Any doubts gone, sky high.

It was true. I hadn't been wrong.

"Did you hear that, Mikey?" I gasped. I let go of his neck but pulled his face close to mine, so I could see that moment when it all fell into place. "Did you hear?"

"Hear what?" he yelled. He pushed me again, livid that I'd manhandled him into the side of a train. "What are you on, for god's sake?"

"You've got to listen!" I said. I could feel my eyes bulging, excited. "To the voice. Can't you hear who it is?"

He shook his head, like I was talking Russian.

"Listen again!" I begged, and the voice cut in, right on cue.

This is Embankment station. Please mind the gap. Change here for the District, Circle and Bakerloo lines.

"Can you not hear?" I shouted again, holding his face so he had to meet my eye. "Who does it sound like?"

"I don't know." He looked baffled. "Like some dick reading the news in the old days. Like a bloke who thinks he's posher than he is."

"Exactly!" I roared. "And who do we know who speaks like that, all the time?"

His face screwed up in confusion.

"I don't know … er …"

"At school, mate, at school."

He shook his head for any answer that would shut me up. "Old man Peach?"

"Exactly. And who did the best impression of Peach we ever heard? Who sounded more like Peach than Peach did?"

At last Mikey stopped and thought. His head stopped shaking, his face uncreased and his eyes opened wider than I thought was possible.

This train is ready to depart. Please mind the closing doors. Stand away from the closing doors.

As if on cue, the doors zoomed in, but not before Mikey tried to ram his fingers between them and hold back the tide.

"No," he yelled. *"No no no – Dad, no.* Don't close, don't close, Dad, don't go."

But the doors were in no mood to listen, no matter how hard he tried to push them apart. After a final, tearful struggle, Mikey had no option but to let them close.

He pressed his palms against the window, so his reflection in the glass made it look like he was praying. As the train pulled away, he ran alongside it, eyes bulging, head shaking, a frantic lover saying goodbye.

I hared along beside him, ignoring the wailing in my ribs.

"It's OK, mate, it's OK," I said. "There's another along in a minute and it'll be exactly the same. I promise."

"But that was him." Mikey's voice was as full as his eyes. "That was Dad, wasn't it? Tell me it was. Tell me you heard it too."

"It is him, mate, it is."

"But how? I don't get it. How did he get on there? How did you find him?"

"By accident," I said. "I was running round town, trying to track down people that knew him. Other actors, his gangster agent, anyone who might have something I could give you. But they had nothing. I was on my way home, working out how to tell you that I'd failed, when I heard him."

"But it's definitely him, isn't it?" Mikey pleaded. "I mean it sounds like him, but it could be someone else, couldn't it?"

I shook my head, and felt a smile on my face for the first time in days.

"I checked, Mikey," I said. "I checked. I went to the office upstairs and I refused to move until they listened to me. They thought I was mental at first, but I wouldn't leave them alone till they contacted someone to find out who the voice belonged to. Then they emailed me this morning and it's definitely your dad. Look, his name's here."

I thrust my phone under Mikey's nose, his eyes flitting across it like he was looking for treasure.

"He recorded it two years ago," I told him. "It's used on every platform in every station on this line. Do you have any idea how many people hear your dad's voice every day? Have you any idea how famous that makes him?"

"And it's definitely him?"

"Yeah! How many actors called Vinny Matthews do you know, mate? Especially ones who do Peach better than Peach?"

I watched Mikey's face as it changed from happy to sad to confused to tearful all in seconds. He looked at the arrivals board, wincing when he saw he had another minute to wait.

"Come on," he whispered, biting at the skin on the side of his thumb.

"It's OK," I reassured him. "It'll still be the same. It'll still be him. I know because I sat here for an hour last night, till I made sure for myself."

We stood together, saying nothing, eyes travelling back and forth to the board, until the dirty breeze began and the tunnel lit up in the distance. We both craned to see even though we knew our wait was almost over.

In raced the train, breathless, reckless. In we leaned as the doors opened. The same voice sounded, but there was a different reaction from Mikey.

"It *is* him, isn't it?" he said. "You can hear it, it's old man Peach all over."

I wrapped my arm round Mikey's shoulder and squeezed gently, feeling him lean in instead of pulling away. Only when the last announcement came, and the doors began to slide shut, did he move, making to walk away again as the train pulled out.

"It's OK, Mikey," I said. "One minute to the next one. That's all. One minute."

So we waited, and we listened. Then we did it again, and again and again. We didn't care what the time was, we didn't care that people looked at us like idiots when we failed, every time, to get on board.

I don't know how many trains came and went. I wasn't counting and it didn't matter, but at last there was a new emotion from Mikey. Tears. Effortless tears. They slid down his face without him once wiping them away, and as they fell, I felt relief.

All right, I know that's messed up. I should probably have cried as well, or comforted him or something, but I couldn't help it. I felt relieved, because as the tears fell, they started to wash away the death mask that had clung to Mikey's face for months. I knew the best thing I could do was stand there, beside my best mate, and watch him cry.

We must have looked a sight. Two crumpled, bruised losers hanging around on a station platform for no reason, one of us crying, the other just watching.

We got plenty of looks, but only one person approached us – an old dear who shuffled our way with a worried look on her face.

"Your mate all right, is he?" she asked in a sing-song voice. "You need some help?"

It was good of her, it really was, and I smiled, despite how much it hurt my face.

"That's kind of you, but it's OK, honest." I looked up one last time at the arrivals board. "His dad will be along in a minute. And he'll sort everything out."

The End

About *Mind The Gap*

I have a lot to thank the X68 bus for.

For six years it ferried me safely to and from work in London, allowing me to avoid the horrors of the Underground.

But that bus did more than just save me from being crammed into a stranger's armpit twice a day – it also became my writing place.

Top deck, front seat, using the window ledge as a luggage rack, I'd manage to bang out 500 words per journey.

Two journeys a day, five days a week, that's ... well, enough words to create a first draft in about six months. (I'm a writer, not a calculator.)

I don't think I've ever been happier writing than when I was on that bus, than when I was constantly looking over my shoulder, anxious that someone was about to pinch my laptop. (Please don't judge me.)

But the X68 didn't just gift me an office, it gifted me ideas too.

The idea for *Mind The Gap* came from an empty seat next to me, from a copy of the *Evening Standard* – the free newspaper – that someone had left there.

Now, I've always thought that the *Standard* is a horrible paper, crammed with bland news and dodgy politics, but for some reason that evening, I was distracted and found myself flicking through it.

It was just about the greatest writing decision I've ever made. There, towards the middle pages, where less important stories go to die, was an article about an old woman whose husband had died. So far, so normal. But as I read on, I became transfixed.

Before his death, the husband had been an actor, and had become the voice of the London Underground – it was his voice that warned commuters to "Mind the gap" as they stepped from their train.

But now, three years after his death, London Underground had started phasing out his voice, much to his wife's distress. As his voice disappeared, her grief increased. It was killing her to hear the final physical evidence of her husband's life disappear.

So she started a campaign, a long campaign, and at last, after many struggles, London Underground agreed to keep this man's voice as the announcement at Embankment station, where his wife still visits regularly, to sit and 'be' with the love of her life.

Sob.

I can't begin to tell you the effect this story had on me. The devotion of this wonderful woman to her husband, the power of her loss, the lengths she went to to keep their love alive, it all moved me profoundly. So much so that I ripped out that article and carried it in my pocket for about a year until it disintegrated.

In that time I read it again and again, never failing to feel goosebumps on my arms. It became clear that it was a story that I wasn't going to forget, so I decided to do something about it. I started to think about how I could take the emotion of it and apply it to the sort of stories I love – stories for teenagers.

And that's when Mikey and his best mate started to appear in my head.

It's probably four or five years since I first read that article, so the story has had plenty of time to develop, but I can honestly say that I've *loved* writing *Mind The Gap*.

When I talk about writing in schools or at festivals, I'm always banging on about there being wonderful drama in the everyday. That fantasy worlds are fabulous, but for me, you can't beat stories that are rooted in the reality of our everyday, often mundane lives. And this story is the perfect example of that.

So I'm really grateful to you for reading *Mind The Gap*, and I really hope it moved you, just like reading that newspaper article moved me.

Acknowledgements

It's a complete thrill to be published by Barrington Stoke – the realisation of a long-held ambition, so I send huge thanks to the team there. To Mairi, Jane, Nina, Kirstin, Julie-ann, Rita, Dominik and of course Emma.

It's an even bigger thrill to have friends who have supported me in the writing of this book, especially Waggy and Tony.

But the biggest thrill is being able to share it with my family – Mum, Dad, Jon, Laura, Albie, Elsie and Stan, who help me mind the gap every single day.

Phil Earle

Hebden Bridge, September 2016

Are you a book eater or a book avoider – or something in between?

This book is designed to help more people love reading. It's a tremendously moving story of being knocked sideways by grief only to be lifted up again by the power of friendship. Unexpected, witty and authentic, *Mind The Gap* is told from the heart by a superstar author. There is plenty here for book lovers to treasure. At the same time, it has clever design features to support more readers.

You may notice the book is printed on heavy paper in two colours – black for the text and a pale yellow Pantone® for the page background. This reduces the contrast between text and paper and hides the 'ghost' of the words printed on the other side of the page. For readers who perceive blur or movement as they read, this may help keep the text still and clear. The book also uses a unique typeface that is dyslexia-friendly.

If you're a book lover, and you want to help spread the love, try recommending *Mind The Gap* to someone you know who doesn't like books. You never know – maybe a super-readable book is all they need to spark a lifelong love of reading.

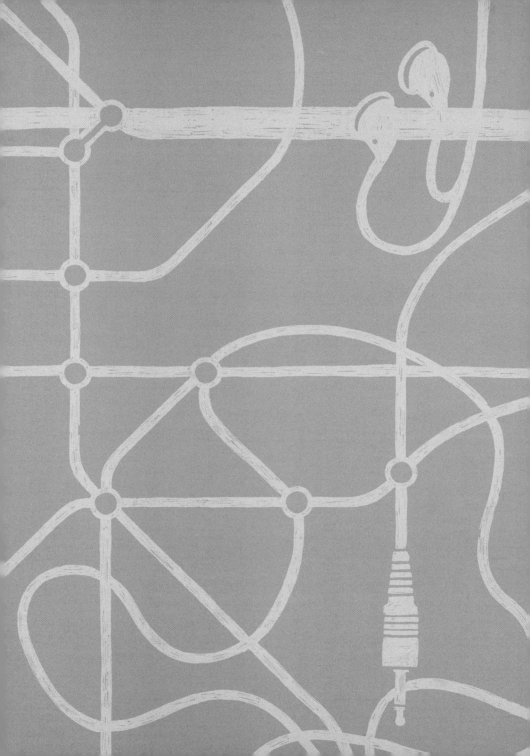